Sister Sun, Brother Storm

Illustrations by Jane Silver
Story by Cynthia Matsakis

First published by Dog Ear Publishing
4010 W. 86th Street, Ste H
Indianapolis, IN 46268
www.dogearpublishing.net

ISBN: 978-1-4575-0768-7

This book is printed on acid-free paper.
This book is a work of fiction. Places, events, and situations in this book are purely
fictional and any resemblance to actual persons, living or dead, is coincidental.

Printed in the United States of America

Amaterasu was the Sun Goddess. She rose each day at dawn to thread her loom with sunbeams, weaving a tapestry of fruit trees and flowers, vegetable patches, wheat fields and rice paddies that covered the earth.

Amaterasu's younger brother was Susanoo, the Storm God, bringer of rain. Wild winds blew as he thundered across the sky. His lightning sword cut the storms loose from the dark heavy clouds. After Susanoo rode past, the earth drank deeply, seeds softened and sprouted.

Susanoo was jealous of his sister. "The people love you more than they love me," he complained. Amaterasu gently rebuked him, "Brother, your lightning sword and reckless storms frighten everyone. You are too excitable, Susanoo. You must tame yourself. A gentle rain will earn you their love."

"Tame myself? Never!" Susanoo shouted. Leaping onto his dark stallion and drawing his lightning sword, he charged recklessly through Amaterasu's peaceful home. Her looms crashed and broke into pieces under the stallion's hooves. The beautiful weavings were torn and tattered. Amaterasu cried out for him to stop but he didn't hear.

Susanoo destroyed the weavings of light, and the world grew dark. As the storm raged on, Amaterasu slipped away to a cave in a distant corner of the world. "Let Susanoo live in his darkness," she said. "I will have none of it."

Amaterasu rested quietly in the silent cave. "I will stay here forever," she decided, "far away from the storm my brother has wreaked upon the world." She rolled a boulder over the mouth of the cave. Now none of her life-giving sunlight could escape.

*S*oon a great frost had covered the land. Vegetables and fruit shriveled on the vine. People grew hungry. Susanoo's angry storm finally ended, but there was no warmth or light, only darkness and shadow. The air was filled with the terrifying screeches of wild birds. Where was Amaterasu?

People wandered the earth in search of her light. Some found their way to her cave and loudly begged her to return. But Amaterasu was silent, thinking to herself, "If I shine brightly again, Susanoo will once more feel jealous and angry. His next storm will be more terrible than the last." She closed her ears to the cries for help.

Amaterasu was haunted by memories of her broken looms and torn tapestries. She had no desire to return to a world where her foolish brother would destroy everything she created. Soon the last of her light faded and she was as dark and silent as her cave.

Susanoo rode alone in the gloomy sky above the forests, overcome by loneliness. In time he began to regret destroying his sister's glorious creation, and finally understood how wrong he was to act out of jealousy and anger. Longing for Amaterasu's light, Susanoo suddenly caught sight of the one tree in the forest that was still green.

The little tree gave Susanoo hope. He carefully loosened its roots from the soil, and took it to the entrance of Amaterasu's cave. He hung hundreds of mirrors all over its beautiful green branches. He thought, "When she looks out, she will see her beauty light up the tree. Then I'll tell her how sorry I am for what I did."

Word of the mirrored tree spread across the land. People came from everywhere to gaze upon it. Musicians brought their instruments, people sang, and a young girl jumped up and danced. Everyone laughed and applauded so loudly that even Amaterasu in her cave heard the joyful sounds.

"What could make them so happy?" she wondered. Amaterasu pushed the boulder aside slightly, just to take a peek, and her light caught on the tree's mirrors, throwing a soft and glowing reflection back into the dark cave. Amaterasu slowly remembered the world as it was before the storm, and decided to try again.

*T*he people cheered as Amaterasu and Susanoo greeted each other. "Sister, without you there is no food, or warmth. It's no wonder that people worship your light." Amaterasu bowed to her brother. "I too have learned something, little brother," she said. "Your rainstorms clear the air, and bring life to seeds. The excitement you create makes us all curious."

Amaterasu and Susanoo both smiled and a bridge of friendship spanned the distance between the light and the storm. Sister and brother began to see how working together brought into being a life-giving balance. Again the earth grew green and golden and the people were grateful to both of them.

CPSIA information can be obtained
at www.ICGtesting.com
Printed in the USA
LVIC06n1038241113
362166LV00002BA/4